Cate:

Merry, Merry

Christmas 2011!

♡,

Mom and Dad

If i could keep you little...

WRITTEN AND ILLUSTRATED BY

Marianne Richmond

sourcebooks
jabberwocky

If i could keep you little...

Published by Sourcebooks Jabberwocky, an imprint of Sourcebooks, Inc.
P.O. Box 4410, Naperville, Illinois 60567-4410
(630) 961-3900
Fax: (630) 961-2168
www.jabberwockykids.com

Library of Congress Cataloging-in-Publication data is on file with the publisher.

Source of Production: Leo Paper, Heshan City, Guangdong Province, China
Date of Production: August 2011
Run Number: 15822

Printed and bound in China.
LEO 10 9 8 7 6 5 4

Also available from author & illustrator Marianne Richmond:

The Gift of an Angel

The Gift of a Memory

Hooray for You!

The Gifts of Being Grand

I Love You So…

Dear Daughter

Dear Son

Dear Granddaughter

Dear Grandson

Dear Mom

Beautiful Brown Eyes

Beautiful Blue Eyes

My Shoes Take Me Where I Want to Go

Fish Kisses and Gorilla Hugs

Happy Birthday to You!

I Love You So Much…

You Are My Wish Come True

Big Sister

Big Brother

If I Could Keep You Little

The Night Night Book

Beginner Boards for the youngest child
simply said… and *smartly said…* mini books
for all occasion

Dedicated to my C, A, J, and W.
I adored you little. And I am in awe
of who you are becoming.
—MR

If I could keep
you little,

I'd **hum** you

lullabies.

But then I'd miss you *singing*

your concert's *big* surprise.

If I could keep you little,

I'd **hold** your hand

everywhere.

But then I'd miss you **knowing,**

"I can go...

you stay there."

If I could keep you little,

I'd **kiss** your
cuts and **scrapes.**

But then I'd miss you *learning* from **your own** mistakes.

If I could
keep you little,

I'd **strap**

you in

real

tight.

But then I'd miss
you *swinging*
from your
treetop height.

If I could
keep you little,

I'd decide on
matching
clothes.

But then I'd miss you **choosing**

GIRL POWER

CHORES
1. Feed Dog
2. Clean Room

The Robot

I ♥ MY DOG

dots on top
***and* stripes below.**

If I could keep you little,

I'd cut your bread into shapes.

But then I'd miss you **finding,**

"Hey! I *like* ketchup

with my grapes!"

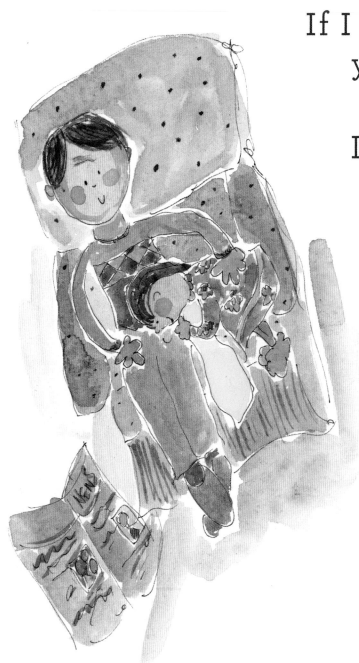

If I could keep
you little,

I'd tell you **stories**
every night.

But then I'd miss
you *reading*

the words
you've learned
by sight.

If I could keep you little,

I'd push you
anywhere.

But then I'd miss you **feeling**

your speed
from *here* to *there!*

If I could keep you little,
I'd pick for you **a friend** or two.

But then I'd miss you **finding**
friends you like *who like you, too!*

If I could keep you little,

we'd **finger-paint** our art.

But then I'd miss you **creating**

stories from

your *heart.*

If I could
keep you little,

I'd push
your *ducky* float.

But then I'd miss you *feeling* the **wind** behind summer's boat.

If I could keep you little,

we'd *nap* in our **fort** midday.

But then I'd miss you **sharing**

adventures from camp **away**.

If I could keep you little, I'd *fly* you *with my* feet.

But then I'd miss you **seeing** **sky and clouds** from your seat.

If I could
keep you little,

I'd keep you
close to me.

But then I'd miss you **growing** into *who you're meant to be!*